For Jane, Hannah and Joe – M.M.
For Chris – E.G.

First published 2021 by Two Hoots an imprint of Pan Macmillan
The Smithson, 6 Briset Street, London, EC1M 5NR

EU representative:
Macmillan Publishers Ireland Limited
Mallard Lodge, Lansdowne Village, Dublin 4

Associated companies throughout the world
www.panmacmillan.com
ISBN 978-1-5290-6331-8

Text copyright © Michael Morpurgo 2021
Illustrations copyright © Emily Gravett 2021
Moral rights asserted.
Music from 'Flight' on pages 2 and 33 copyright © Rachel Portman 2020,
reproduced by kind permission
A version of this story first appeared in *The Book of Hopes*,
edited by Katherine Rundell, published by Bloomsbury Publishing plc

1 3 5 7 9 8 6 4 2
A CIP catalogue record for this book is available from the British Library.
Printed in Poland
The illustrations in this book were created
using pencil and watercolour with a smidgen of digital fiddle faddling

www.twohootsbooks.com

MIX
Paper from
responsible sources
FSC® C116313
FSC
www.fsc.org

MICHAEL MORPURGO   EMILY GRAVETT

A Song of Gladness

TWO HOOTS

I'VE BEEN TALKING
every morning to blackbird,
   telling him why we are all so sad.
   He sits on his branch and listens.

It was blackbird's idea. He sang it out this morning
at dawn from his treetop in the garden, to fox half asleep
behind the garden shed. She thought it a good idea too.
It was a wake-up call. Fox was on her feet at once, and
trotting through Bluebell Wood, where she barked it to
deer who ran off across the stream.

Kingfisher was there, otter and dipper too.
They heard, and piped it on, and swallow
swooped down over the meadow,

and passed it on to cows waiting to go in to their milking, and to sheep resting quietly under the hedge with her lambs in the corner of the dew-damp field.

And they all agreed, bleating it out to bees already busy at their flowers, to weaving spiders, and grasshoppers, and scurrying mice.

Trees were listening too, all the trees, waving their budding leaves in wild enthusiasm.

High above in the skies,
clouds gathered, driven by wind,

and wind took blackbird's idea over the cliffs across heaving seas,
where gulls and albatross cried it out, and whales and dolphins
and porpoises heard it, and wailed and whooped it down into
the deep, where turtles listened. And they too loved the idea.

So did plankton and every fish and crab and sea urchin
and whelk. They all whispered that it was a fine notion,
the best they ever heard.

In rivers, salmon and sea trout leapt for joy to hear it. Eagles soaring above on wide wings flew over the mountains crying it out loud, and the echoes were heard deep in the dens below, where slumbering bears listened, lost in their dreams of spring. They snored and grunted their approval, even in their sleep.

Snows melted at the thought of it, and the whole wonderful idea flooded down the mountain streams and far out to sea, where the tide took it and carried it over the sea on curling waves to distant shores, to parched plains, where lions roared their approval, and elephants trumpeted it, leopards yawned it,

water buffalo belched it, wild dogs yelped it.
And wildebeest murmured it out across the wide savannah.

Then storm lifted the idea up over rainforests,
where rain took it and poured it down on gorillas
in the mist, on chimpanzees in their sleeping nests.

And crocodile swished his tail in his swamp,
and clapped his great jaws shut, smiling at
the very thought of it.

Howler monkeys and gibbons echoed their calls loud over all the earth – they are that loud; and then from far up high, sun heard it too and shone it down over deserts where oryx stamped her foot, impatient to be getting on with it and doing it – she loved the idea that much.

Even camel, who rarely joined in anything, thought this was the best and most beautiful idea he had ever heard.

Back in the garden,
blackbird waited till everyone was ready.

And then he began to sing. The whole carnival of animals heard him and every living thing on this good earth joined in, until the globe echoed with the joy of it.

Blackbird was very pleased.

But I was still lost in sadness, as I heard the earth singing around me. It was a song of forgiveness. I knew that. So I asked blackbird if I was allowed to join in. And he sang his answer back to me.

"My friend, why do you think we are doing this? We want you and yours to be happy again. Only then will you treat us and the world right, as you know you should. Only then will all be well. Sing, my friend, sing. Our song is your song, your song is our song."

So I sang, we all sang, sang away our sadness.

In every house and flat and cottage, we clapped and sang, in every shelter and tent, in every palace and hospital and prison. And they heard and we heard, our song of gladness echoing about us, in glorious harmony across the universe.

And one more thing …

For some years now I've been going out early every morning into the vegetable garden to pick kale or spinach, raspberries or gooseberries (my favourite). I was out there one lovely bright morning in March 2020, the year all of us will remember for the rest of our lives, a time of such sorrows.

There was not a cloud in the sky and all about me a silence so intense that I could hear it. The world seemed to have stopped. I felt I was alone on the planet. There was such beauty all around me, such peace. I should have been happy on such a morning, but instead I was overwhelmed with sadness.

Then a blackbird began to sing.

I knew at once he was singing to me, that this was personal. Sensing his welcome, I sang back, echoing his song. We had a conversation. It sounds fanciful. At first, I thought it was fanciful. But when he was there waiting for me, singing for me, every morning, I knew he was trying to get to know me, to tell me something, something important – urgent even.

He was telling me a story, singing a song he wanted the whole world to sing, every living creature on the planet.

As I stood there listening, I felt he wanted me to write it down, to pass it on. I wrote it the same day and read it out to him the next morning. He sang me his applause. I sang back my thanks. We had done it together. I have never felt a closer sense of belonging to the world about me.

It is a world that generations of us have been, and are still, destroying, with our speed and our greed. It is up to us to change that, the future of the planet depends on us. But first we have to care, to feel that each one of us is part of this earth, that this earth is precious and fragile, that every plant and creature matters as much as we do. But we will not care unless we feel we belong, and to do that we need to know the wild world about us at first hand, to walk in it, breathe it in, marvel at it, to know we are all part of the same earth. This song of gladness is for everyone, to bring hope, and to cheer us on our way as we learn to care together for our planet.

By the way, my blackbird is back. I heard him again this morning. I told him that he was here in this book, singing his song, and he flew off to tell all his friends in the garden. And tomorrow morning I know he'll be back. I'll still be here waiting for him, listening for his song of gladness.